10·5·95 Forest House 13.00

10/19/23 ØCORE
1 √out march '20
withdraw

Read on, Rita

written by
Stephen Cosgrove

Illustrated by
Wendy Edelson

Carousel

Read on, Rita is dedicated to the 3R's: Ruth, Rebecca, and Rachel, my three reading Ritas. Three magical minds daring to dream in the land of Barely There.

Stephen

AN IMPRINT OF FOREST HOUSE™

This 1993 School and Library Edition published by FOREST HOUSE PUBLISHING COMPANY, INC.

Publisher
Nancy L. Cosgrove
Editor
J. Matthew Stuart
Technical Editor
Susan Lanctot

Read on, Rita
© 1992 by Stephen E. Cosgrove
Published by
The Carousel™

13110 NE 177th PL
Woodinville, WA 98072

Printed proudly in the United States of America

Library of Congress Cataloging–in–Publication Data

Cosgrove, Stephen.
    Read on, Rita / by Stephen Cosgrove ; illustrated by
Wendy Edelson.
    p. cm.
    Summary: Rita, a young raccoon discovers that all the books in the land are being bought by a sly hedgehog who firmly believes a picture is worth a thousand words, Rita, in a competition, convinces him that from words come great dreams and pictures.

    HTS Library Binding   ISBN 1-56674-042-8
    (1. Reading–Fiction 2. Literacy–Fiction 3. Animals–Fiction) I. Title

In the United States today, one out of every five women is functionally illiterate. Many cannot read a newspaper, enjoy a book, or follow the instructions on a job application. They have never found the magic of words and the delightful pictures that can be painted with them. We want to help, which is why we're sending the proceeds from this book to women's literacy projects across the country. We hope children will enjoy *Read On Rita* and will come to understand how special the gift of literacy is for everyone.

We thank you for sharing Rita's story and her inspiration. Together, we can keep the joys of reading alive.

Peter H. Coors

Stephen Cosgrove

Coors

LITERACY. PASS IT ON.

Farther than far and to the very edge of the horizon was a path bordered by lacy fern. If you scurried down that path following a buzzing bumble bee – its tiny legs weighted in the golden pollen of red-red rose – you would find the land of Barely There.

Barely There... where words and
pictures are woven together with blossoms and willow vine.
Barely There... where the Fuzzy Folk live. Here, T.J. Flopp,
Fiddler Bear, and Persimmony patiently wait for you wrapped
in the pages of stories gone by softly whispering.... Barely
There, Barely There.

Hurry now, follow that bee down the path as it buzzes and weaves from side to side.

Scurry now, as the bee turns this way and that, winging home to honey and hive.

Look there! Home at last to a buzzing hive hanging from the limb of a tree.

Beyond honeycomb and winging bees, there lay a quaint little village. Here, cozy cottages were clustered about the only store – WORDWORTHY'S FEED, SEED AND MERCANTILE.

This mercantile, this store, was a place of great learning – a place of books and imagination. This was the place where children and adults alike came to buy a persimmon or a plum and to read books from the library. Big books, little books, and picture books – were all read and re-read, cherished by the minds of the creatures who lived here.

Everyone in the Land of Barely There read and those who didn't were helped by tutors – reading helpers who guided those not fortunate enough to have gained the skills they needed in school. Ira Wordworthy, the owner of the store and once a non–reader himself, was a tutor. Rita, a young raccoon who delighted in brightening the lives of others was a tutor. All the tutors, all the volunteers were special. Each had reached out to help someone who didn't know how to read.

Today, Rita sat in the warmth of the sun helping Hannah and Hickory, the Heart twins, read a borrowed book from the library. This time, as the last, the twins didn't bring their own books to read. When they were finished reading, Rita curiously asked, "Why don't you bring your own books anymore?"

They smiled sweet cream smiles and happily mewed, "Oh, we traded them for pictures. With pictures you don't need to read. You just look at the story."

"Oh, no!" admonished Rita. "The pictures are there to help with the words, not to replace them."

The reading lesson over, Hannah and Hickory scampered away leaving Rita to ponder this dilemma. "Hmm," she thought, "I must find out who is trading books for pictures, and why?"

With that she set out to find this trader of books.

She searched the Land of Barely There seeking the trader, but no trader did she find. Instead what she found were the children carrying delightful bits of painted imagination. They carried pictures of unicorns, fairies and all sorts of forest folk. Each picture was signed in the same odd way – 'picture and dreams by Nettles B. Nebbish.'

Odder than odd was the fact that the children, in turn, told Rita they didn't have to read books any more. They all said that Nettles had told them each of his pictures was worth a thousand words – one book. Now knowing the cause of their disinterest in reading, Rita went in search of the mysterious painter, Nettles B. Nebbish.

She didn't have to look far. She didn't have to look hard. A steady stream of children wound down a path that ended in a very quiet spot in the Land of Barely There. Here, in an abandoned brambled hedge in a bower of flowering laurel, Rita found the infamous painter and trader of pictures... Nettles B. Nebbish.

Nettles was a peculiar sight indeed. It was only fitting that he should live in the laurel, for he was a hedgehog of dubious distinction. His hair shot up from his head in wild spikes. He wore a blousy shirt tucked into baggy pants and wore no shoes what-so-ever. He was splattered with paint from head to foot and a molehair brush was tucked behind his left ear.

Nettles stood in the shelter of his hedge and with each child he traded a picture for a book. To each he repeated in his squeaky little voice, "Remember, you don't need to read! A picture is worth a thousand words!" Stacked and strewn about him on the path were the abandoned books no longer wanted by the children.

He stood there looking at Rita who was standing there looking at him. "Well," said he, "I suppose you too have come for a painting." In his fuzzy, little paint-splotched hands he held the most beautiful picture Rita had ever seen.

Rita was so taken with the picture that she nearly forgot her intent and meekly asked, "Wherever did you find such a marvelous sight to paint?"

"Ah, my little raccoon, that is my secret – a secret never shared."

"It is a beautiful picture," sighed Rita, "but I don't know if it's worth a book. After all, you can't read a picture!"

Nettles smiled a twisted hedgehog smile and slyly said, "Reading is for sissies! Why don't you take the picture. It will only cost you a thousand words – just one little book."

"Bu–but," stammered Rita, "if you take all of the books in exchange for pictures, soon the children won't remember how to read. If they forget how to read they will forget how to dream."

The little hedgehog cocked his head and smiled a painted smile. "Oh poppycock! You just don't get it, do you little raccoon? Well, let me explain. When all the books are gone I shall be rich beyond measure. You see, the children who don't learn to read and those who forget how to read will have to buy my pictures. I'll charge them just a little bit, and a little bit will add up to a lot... a lot of money, money, money. I will be a very rich hedgehog indeed."

"That's not fair!" exclaimed Rita.

"Fair," he squealed, "I'll give you fair." With that he rifled through his paintings and finally held out one small picture to Rita. It was a pretty picture of a tiny little baby, wrapped in a bright pink blanket, cradled on the branch of a tree. "Fair is: you find this tree, my source of inspiration for this painting and I'll stop trading pictures for books. Then, you can save the children's precious little dreams. But you must find the exact tree in one day's time."

Rita looked at the picture and quietly asked, "And if I can't find the tree?"

"Then," slyly replied Nettles, "you shall give me all of your books and promise never to read – ever again."

Rita didn't know what to do. She loved to read more than anything in the whole world. She looked at the picture. She looked at Nettles B. Nebbish. Finally she extended her hand and said, "I accept. I will take your challenge."

The little hedgehog turned his head from side-to-side. Cautious was he, as he scrunched his eyes and smiled a mischievous smile. With that, he shook her hand in his paint-smudged paw.

The challenge had begun.

21

Rita turned from the laurel and walked away looking about for the tree she had seen painted in Nettles' picture. No matter where she searched, she couldn't find the illustrated tree that cradled a child in its boughs.

Finally, she hurried, skirts dancing in the dust, back to Wordworthy's store.

The store was quite empty, save for Ira sitting all alone on a bag of seed near the blackened, potbelly stove. Ira often sat near the stove reading a book. But today, the old badger was idly staring at his great paws, turning them this way and that as if some great treasure was buried beneath his claws. Today there was something different, for there was no book in his hand and no books were close by.

"How come you are not reading a book?" she curiously asked.

"Just because," said Ira with a great sigh. "Because there is nothing to read and I, uh, well, ahem... I traded all of my books for pictures."

"Oh, Ira," she cried, "not you, too!"

Sure enough, if you looked about the store, the walls were covered with paintings all signed the same; "picture and dreams by Nettles B. Nebbish."

Sadly, Rita explained Nettles' plan to take all the books from the Land of Barely There. Together they studied the small picture she held – the picture of the baby cradled in the tree top. They looked and they looked. Never had they seen a tree quite like this, but still the picture seemed ever so familiar.

They studied all afternoon. They studied into the night. At half past dark they lit candles and oil lamps and continued to ponder the picture. Their study was disturbed as the bell clanged above the door. In skittered the odd little painter himself – Nettles B. Nebbish.

"Ah, my little wordly raccoon," he crooned. "Find the answer yet? My pile of books grows higher and higher – thousands and thousands of words. Ha! Ha!"

"I think I know the answer," she bluffed, "The tree is near old Fiddler's cabin and you placed the baby in the tree so you could paint your picture."

"Nope!" giggled the hedgehog as he popped a cracker into his mouth. "That's not it!"

On and on, Rita and Ira tried to discover Nettle's source of inspiration. To each of their solutions Nettles simply answered, "Nope!" and then ate another cracker.

They sought the answer all through the night and into the dawn. With the sun cresting above the trees, Nettles yawned a painter's yawn, "See ya soon little raccoon. I'll be back later to pick up all of your books." Brushing the cracker crumbs from his hair, he scurried out the door.

Rita and Ira were left alone except for the echo of the bell. They each sat on a bag of seed, their chins propped in their furry hands. They looked straight ahead hoping an answer would come walking through the door. Strangely enough, it did.

The bell clanged again as in walked a dusty little miner; a tiny little shrew called Shelby. Shelby, like most shrews, was light–blind. She couldn't see a thing in the bright light of day. She walked into the mercantile, tapping a cane before her.

"Good morning, Ira," softly spoke the shrew, turning her head to one side listening for his voice.

"It's not such a good morning, Shelby," said Ira as he sadly explained what had happened.

"I can help you," said the little miner brightly. "I can see in my mind the picture your words will paint. If you tell me the story of the painting I'm sure I can find the tree."

Rita began telling the story of the picture. She described a little baby asleep in a cradle nestled in the bough of a tree. She richly told how the cradle and the baby seemed to be rocking gently in the wind. The little shrew stood there, her chin resting on her cane, smiling and bobbing her head as the words drew a picture in her mind.

Then, just like that, Rita knew the answer! She dashed from the store and was gone but a moment or two. She returned clutching a book from the library in her hand – a tiny, tattered book. In the book was the source of Nettles' inspiration: the answer to the riddle. The hedgehog had simply painted a picture of a story, a nursery rhyme called Rock–A–Bye Baby. Nettles had colorfully illustrated a book, a story already written, for art in books is drawn like a map for young minds to follow.

With the riddle solved Nettles B. Nebbish would be forced to give back the thousands of words for which he had unfairly traded. He would have to give the children back their books. He would have to give the children back their dreams.

Wrapped in the magic of the moment, Ira, Shelby, and Rita whirled about the store singing,

"READ ON, RITA, READ ON.
READ ON, RITA, READ ON.
BOOKS ARE THE KEY,
DREAMS YOU CAN SEE.
READ ON, RITA, READ ON."

And Rita did read on and on and on. From her books came great dreams and from her dreams – greater tomorrows... in the Land of Barely There.

Stephen Edward Cosgrove

Stephen was born July 26, 1945 in Spokane, Washington and has written over two hundred books. He now lives with his beloved wife Nancy, his delightful step-son Matthew, his little dog Rhubarb, his attack cat Snickers and two gold fish the size of whales in the foothills of the Cascade Mountains near Seattle, Washington.

Other books by Stephen Cosgrove

Treasure Trolls
The Snuffin Chronicles
Woodcarver
Dream Stealer
Balderdash
The Serendipity Books
The Books From Barely There